William is a small two wheel drive tractor he spends most of his time in the yard scraping out muck, spreading straw in the sheds and feeding the animals. Occasionally Farmer Fields needs William to do some work in the fields, which he loves. He longs to be like his older brothers James and Henry; William is a good tractor most of the time but he can get up to mischief occasionally, especially if he's with Henry!

It was a hot and sunny morning on Faraway Farm, **Colin the Combine** was hard at work cutting a field of wheat for **Farmer Fields**. Not only was the harvest underway but **Munch the Mower** had cut a field of grass a few days earlier. The grass had been spread by **Ted the Spreader** and left to dry in the sun.

Henry had been given the job of rowing up the dried grass into rows. He hitched up Row the Rake and was making his way to middle field. As he drove out of the yard he passed William who had just finished scraping out the sheds.

"Hello William" said Henry, "Row and I are going to middle field to row-up the hay"

"what's row-up?" replied a confused William.

"I rake up the grass into rows now that it's dry, so that Smally the Baler can bale it" shouted Row from behind Henry.

I wonder if I'll be needed to help thought William as Henry drove off with Row.

William felt very excited because he did not get to work in the fields very often; most of his time was spent working in the yard and sheds. As William was driving back to the yard he met Farmer Fields and JP. "It's going to be a very busy day William, I'm going to need you to help in the field, do you think you can do that?" "Oh yes please Farmer Fields", replied William. Farmer Fields explained that James and Ronald the Round Baler were going to round bale the wheat straw once Colin had finished cutting. Henry was going to hitch up Smally the Small Square Baler and bale the hay, once he had finished rowing-up the hay with Row. So Farmer Fields needed William to pick up a trailer of bales from each field once they had been loaded by Telly the Telescopic Loader.

William was so excited that he was going to be working in the field that he forgot which fields the hay and straw were in. Later in the day when **William** had finished all his jobs he headed out of the yard and trundled down the track to the fields. **William** was looking for a stack of bales and he soon spotted them parked in the corner of long field. He quickly drove into the field to find **Luke the Low Loader** with a full stack of bales.

"**Hello Luke** I've come to take you back to the yard" said **William**. "Do you know what bales you are stacked with?" "No sorry **William** I don't, I do know that they are round bales" replied **Luke**. **William** hitched up **Luke** and drove back to the yard. The problem was he could not remember whether **Farmer Fields** had said that the round bales were the hay or straw bales.

William reversed **Luke** back into the Barn and was about to head back out into the field when he saw Choppsy the Straw Chopper. **William** explained his problem of not knowing the difference between hay and straw to **Choppsy**. "It's simple" said **Choppsy** "hay is dried grass that we feed to the animals and being grass it's green. Straw is the stem of a crop once it's been through the combine harvester and had the seed removed it's mostly yellow. We use this to make the animals beds with".

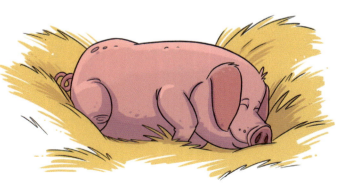

"Thanks **Choppsy**" said **William**. He raced out of the yard he knew where he was going now. The round bales he brought back were yellow and he used those bales to bed down the animals. The hay bales he had to collect were dried grass so they must be at the grass field. **William** arrived at square field to find **Telly** loading the last bale onto **Holly the hay trailer**. "Is everything ok?" **William** said **Telly**. "It is now" said **William** "I now know the difference between hay and straw, and I don't think I'll ever get muddled up again"!

For more information on the adventures at The Faraway Farm visit

www.thefarawayfarm.com

"Book two in the Faraway Farm series to follow soon"

Printed in Great Britain
by Amazon